The Snowman

by Simon Gaspard
illustrated by Carolyn Croll

Strategy Focus

As we read this story, let's think about how to make a snowman.

 HOUGHTON MIFFLIN   BOSTON

Here is the snow.
We like the snow.

Here are the rocks.
We like the rocks.

Here is a carrot.
We like the carrot.

Here are the sticks.
We like the sticks.

Here is a hat.
We like the hat.

Here is a scarf.
We like the scarf.

Here is the snowman.
We like the snowman!